GHOST STORIES
TO SCARE YOUR SOCKS OFF!

EDITED BY BENJAMIN BIRD

raintree

a Capstone company — publishers for children

Raintree is an imprint of Capstone Global Library Limited, a company incorporated in England and Wales having its registered office at 264 Banbury Road, Oxford, OX2 7DY – Registered company number: 6695582

www.raintree.co.uk
myorders@raintree.co.uk

Designed by Kay Fraser and Tracy Davies
Design elements by Shutterstock/Nadia Chi
Cover and interior illustrations by Andi Espinosa

978 1 3982 5492 3

British Library Cataloguing in Publication Data
A full catalogue record for this book is available from the British Library.

Printed and bound in India

CONTENTS

THE GHOST OF CAMP MONROE

BY BENJAMIN HARPER

I was already scared of ghosts. I swore I'd seen one when I was younger, hovering over my bed. My mum told me it was just my imagination and to get back to sleep – but how could I when this ghost was inches away from my face?

I hadn't seen any ghosts since then, but here I was at Camp Monroe, away from home for the first summer ever. We were sitting round the fire after supper, making s'mores, when a counsellor called Jason started telling us a story.

"Years and years ago," he started, "a boy drowned in our lake. They searched and searched, but they never found his body."

Everyone around the fire inched a little closer. Jason paused for effect, holding his hands up. "And now," he continued, "they say the waters of the lake are haunted. People say they can feel his presence in the lake when they're swimming. Some even claim to have seen or felt him!"

"How are we supposed to go swimming after this?" I said, but everyone around me just laughed.

"Don't be such a baby," a girl called Angela said. "Yeah, ghosts aren't real," another camper called Ricky added. But Jason shushed them.

"The ghost is real, alright. I've seen it," Jason said spookily. "The boy's mother comes out every year on the anniversary of his death and calls to him, hoping he'll appear, but he never does."

"When is the anniversary?" I asked, making a note

to stay away from the lake on that particular day.

"Tomorrow!" Jason said.

"TOMORROW?" I cried. "Tomorrow is the big race to see who the fastest swimmer is! How can it be tomorrow?" I loved swimming. In fact, it was my favourite thing in the world. I didn't want a ghost to ruin it.

"That's why I'm telling you now," Jason said, getting very serious. "When you're out in that water, if you feel anything funny, you'd better swim for your life – the ghost of the drowned camper is after you!"

Great. How was I supposed to get any sleep after hearing that? Getting into the lake would be twice as hard tomorrow, knowing there was a spirit under the water that was going to try to scare us.

As hard as it was after hearing that spooky story, I finally fell asleep. I woke up feeling fresh and ready for the swimming competition – that is, until I remembered the Ghost of Lake Monroe! What if he attacked me while I was doing the backstroke?

We made our way down to the shore of the lake, where I saw an old woman standing on the dock. She was looking out over the water. I knew just who she was as soon as I saw her.

We were taking our positions when I started shaking. "I can't do it," I whimpered. "I can't swim in that lake after what you told us last night!"

Jason came over to me, a smile on his face. "That was just a ghost story! I made it up. There's no ghost in the lake, I promise you."

"Then who is that lady?" I said, pointing over to the woman on the dock. "She's looking for him!"

"That's Mrs Christie," Jason told me. "She was the swimming champion in 1970. She comes back every year to judge the competition – she lives just up the road."

"Really?" I asked. I wasn't sure I believed him.

"Really. If you want, we can go and ask her."

I didn't want to look any more like a baby than I already did, so I decided to believe what he was telling me.

Back in the line, we waited in position, bent over and ready to dive into the lake. We had to swim to the other side of the area and back. It was a lot! But I knew I could do it.

"Get ready, get set..." Jason paused. "GO!"

We all dived into the water. I already felt good about this race. I was doing freestyle, and I was going really fast!

Then, halfway across the lake, I felt something under the water, like a hand trying to grab my leg. It happened once, twice...

"It's just some plants or a log," I told myself. Jason had promised there was no ghost.

Then a girl screamed! I looked behind me, and she was bobbing in the water. "It grabbed me!" she shouted. She started treading water frantically, splashing everywhere.

I couldn't lose concentration. I wanted to win.

But then it happened. I felt a hand grab my foot. It actually pulled me underwater! I scrambled to get back to the surface. I kicked and paddled and pulled. Finally, I broke the surface.

"Was it him?" I saw the old woman on the dock shouting. "Was it my boy?!?" She ran to the edge of the dock, crying out to me. "Did you see him?"

After that, I swam faster than I ever had in my entire life. So fast, in fact, that I won. I got to the shore first. I ran as far away from the water as possible and looked over at the dock. I vowed never to set foot in a lake ever again in my entire life!

Jason stood next to the old woman with his mouth open.

When everyone was finally back on the shore, we shivered and stared out at the water. We saw bubbles and ripples moving across its surface. Then an eerie presence raised out of the water and floated away.

"That's him, alright," the old woman said. "I knew I'd find him again."

THE NIGHTMARE

BY LAURIE S. SUTTON

It was after midnight, but Professor Len Abbey was still working at his desk. The room was dark. The only light came from a single lamp and the glow of a computer screen. The professor hardly noticed. He was wrapped up in his research. He was writing a book about dreams.

Stacks of old books were piled on the desk. Other books lay open. They all had dozens of pages bookmarked with scraps of paper and sticky notes. The computer displayed at least as many open tabs and windows.

Tap-tap-tap. The professor typed some notes and thoughts into a document. His fingers were stiff with old age. After a while, the professor's focus started to fade. His eyelids drooped. He could not hold back a yawn. He fought the urge to sleep, but sleep won. Professor Abbey began to dream.

"Hello! Here you are at last!" a woman said. She was dressed in a little girl's party dress but she was not a little girl. She was an adult woman. He couldn't remember her name, but he knew her anyway.

"Sorry if I'm late," the professor replied. It seemed natural to say this. He felt like he was supposed to be here. Wherever "here" was. He looked around. He was in a room with a lot of people. They all wore pointed party hats.

"Happy birthday, Len," the woman said.

The people in the room gathered around him. They smiled and said things he couldn't really understand. Their words blurred together. He saw friends from his school days who had not aged a bit.

They looked as young as they had back then. He was very happy to see his friend Chris. That's when the professor knew he was dreaming. Chris had died many years ago. Still, it was good to see him.

The woman in the little girl's party dress put her hand on the professor's arm and walked him over to a table. It was piled high with birthday presents, bowls of ice cream, sweets and a huge cake. There seemed to be a hundred candles on the cake.

"Ha, ha! I'm not that old!" The professor laughed when he saw all of the candles.

Someone put a slice of cake in his hand, even though no one had cut the cake. He hadn't even blown out the candles. The professor took a bite but couldn't taste anything. In the back of his mind, he knew that this was normal in dreams.

The room gradually grew darker around him. His surroundings became fuzzy, like being in a fog. The sound of voices faded. The party guests were still there, but now they all wore masks. Weird, scary masks. Bird beaks and scowls. Snarls and snake fangs.

The professor didn't recognize his friends any more. He tried to back away, to turn round and leave. But there was no way out. No exit. Only dark fog.

The guests circled around him. Closed in on him. He was alarmed when they grabbed him and lifted him over their heads. He tried to squirm out of their grasp, but he couldn't move his limbs. It was as if his body was wrapped in an invisible blanket. They took him over to the table and put him on top of it.

"What? What's happening?!" the professor tried to shout, but only a whisper came out of his mouth.

The party guests leaned over the professor as he lay stretched out on the table. They didn't wear masks any more. Their faces had changed into terrible, twisted shapes. They reached towards him with hideous hands. Claws. Talons.

Fear shot through Professor Abbey's body. His dream had turned into a nightmare!

He wanted to wake up but he couldn't move. Then he realized why. His body had turned into cake. He was covered in icing. And then the ghostly beings started to eat him! They licked the icing with long, slimy tongues. They dug into him with their claws and stuffed their faces. They tore at him in a feeding frenzy.

"Noooo!" the professor screamed just before they ate his face.

* * *

Professor Abbey's assistant came into his office the next morning and found him slumped in his chair. His body was limp. Motionless. He looked like he was asleep. She checked. He wasn't.

"Oh, Professor," she said sadly as she called the emergency services. "It's too bad you didn't get to finish writing your book. But at least you died peacefully, in your sleep. I hope you had pleasant dreams."

THE MAN IN THE HAT

BY MICHAEL DAHL

Rita saw the man in the hat in the alley behind their house. It was dark outside, and she was returning home from her friend Sally's house a few streets away. Rita had walked this way dozens of times. The only thing different that night was the cold. An icy breeze coursed around corners and rushed over roofs. Rita zipped her jacket up to her chin.

Rita was about to turn into the alley that led to the back of her house. That's when she saw him. A man's tall shadow appeared on a neighbour's garage wall, facing her. He wore a tall hat that reminded Rita of a magician's hat. A hat where a rabbit or bouquet of flowers could pop out at any time. It sat above the man's head like a tall, thick tree trunk.

Rita stopped. If the man's shadow was this tall, wouldn't the man himself be taller? Like a giant? Maybe not. Rita remembered when she and her twin brother, Stan, played with a torch in her bedroom. They made monsters move on the wall using their fingers' shadows. The monsters grew larger the closer they held the torch to their hands.

The man must be standing close to a light in the alleyway.

The man's shadow grew larger. His tall hat stretched above the garage roof.

Then, he reached out with a pale, skinny hand.

The man's fingers moved along the garage wall like figures on a cinema screen. Like the shadows Rita and Stan had made in her bedroom. The crooked fingers stretched closer to the end of the alley where Rita was standing.

"Who is that?" Rita called out. "Who's there?"

She stepped off the pavement into the middle of the alley. No one else was there.

The shadowy man and his tall hat were still sliding along the neighbour's wall. But Rita saw nothing making the shadow. There wasn't even a light for a man to be standing in front of. The only lights came from the windows of other neighbours' houses.

Somewhere a dog barked. The tall man and his tall hat disappeared. Rita glanced up and down the alley. *Something had made that shadow, right?* she told herself. Shadows don't appear out of nowhere.

The girl ran down the alley until she reached the back gate into her garden. She hurried inside the house, ran into her bedroom and shut the door. *What's wrong with me?* Rita wondered. *Am I really afraid of a stupid shadow?* Besides, it was only a man's shadow. A man with a strangely tall hat that could grow.

Rita took off her jacket and hat. She still felt cold, a bitter breeze blew through her room. Her window was open. The curtains fluttered like ghostly hands. Rita walked closer. She frowned because she knew she hadn't left it open. Maybe Stan had opened it. But he knew better. He knew that he was never allowed in her room without her permission.

Rita looked out of the window. The alley could be clearly seen from her bedroom. As she watched in silent terror, a man's tall, slender shadow was stretched along the surface of the alleyway. The hat was growing again. The hat shadow disappeared behind the edge of her family's garage. But then it appeared on the garage wall nearest the house.

It moved along the pavement leading up to their back door. Still, Rita couldn't see the man who was making the shadow.

She slammed her window shut and locked it. She pulled the curtains shut. No light shone in her room except for the lamp next to her bed.

Something knocked at her door. It slowly opened. "Rita?" called her brother.

Rita pulled the door open all the way. "Were you in my room?" she demanded.

Stan shook his head. "No, I wasn't," he said.

"Well, *someone* was," said Rita. "They left the window wide open. You could have let anything inside. Like moths or leaves or —"

Stan stepped further into the room. Rita could tell he was holding something behind his back.

"I think my friend opened it," Stan said.

"Your friend?"

Stan pulled a hat from behind his back. It was black and shiny and smooth. And tall. It looked exactly like a magician's hat. The same hat the shadow man was wearing.

Dark mist oozed from the hat's opening. It spilled into the bedroom and grew quickly like a sudden thunderstorm. Stan was gone. Instead, Rita saw the hat was being held by the man-shaped shadow. Her bedroom was growing darker and darker.

"Rita!" came her brother's voice. He sounded far away. "Look!" he cried. "My friend's hat is so cool. He wants us to come inside."

Rita backed up against the window.

"It's beautiful in here," said Stan.

She started to scream. Then her bedroom light blinked out. Rita kept screaming but now sounded tiny and far away.

From even further away came her brother's

dwindling voice. "Can you see it, Rita?" he asked. "Can you see it?"

A GRIM DECISION

BY MEGAN ATWOOD

Antonia looked down the pitch and saw her best friend and teammate ready to run for the ball. She kicked it hard past the defence and watched as Skylar sprinted past them, tapping the ball from Antonia's perfect pass and then kicking it into the goal. Just then, the referee blew her whistle to signal the end of the match.

Antonia's whole team gathered around Skylar and hugged her fiercely, whooping and smiling and laughing. Antonia joined in, though she felt a little jealous. It had been from her pass, after all.

But it didn't matter: the Thornton Tigers had won their first match, and now they would be advancing in the tournament. It made the trip to a new town totally worth it. Antonia felt a huge swell of pride and love for her whole team. They were going to win this tournament. They all lined up to shake hands with the opposing team – the Roscoe Red Devils – and they went down the line. A couple of the girls from the Devils team sniggered.

Antonia and Skylar shared a look. This wouldn't be the first time another team was jealous of them.

"Good luck in your changing rooms," one of the Devils said, laughing.

Antonia felt her eyebrows furrow. "The changing rooms?" she said, before she could stop herself.

"Yeah. Hope you make it out alive," the girl said, still laughing. The shaking hands was done, so Antonia didn't have time to say anything back.

Skylar put her arm around her. "They're just

jealous they can't work together as well as we can," she said. Antonia nodded, and the team walked to the changing rooms they had been assigned.

As they walked in, Antonia swore she felt something cold pass through her. She shivered. One of her teammates said, "Ooooh, this changing room is so scary!" The whole team laughed, including Antonia. But Antonia felt like it really was.

The lights overhead flickered. Somehow, what light there was couldn't chase away the shadows in the corner of the room. But soon the girls chatted, and the scariness of the locker room seemed to drift away.

Suddenly, Gabrielle said, "*Shh*. Do you hear that?"

The team went quiet. From the other room, they heard a shower running and someone singing an eerie song. Skylar and Antonia looked at each other with wide eyes. Without even speaking, the team moved towards the shower room and turned the corner. All the showers were going at once – no one was there.

As they stood watching, the locker doors in the other room slammed shut. Antonia jumped and screamed with the rest of the team. Except for Skylar.

She put her hands on her hips and said, "OK, losers, funny prank. Pretty bad sports, aren't you?" There was no answer except the sound of the showers running.

Antonia relaxed. This made the most sense. They were getting pranked. One of her teammates went around and turned off all the shower nozzles, muttering about it being bad for the environment. The team moved back to the locker part of the changing rooms and changed into their clothes.

Nothing else happened, and Antonia began to relax even more. One by one, the teammates left until it was just Skylar and Antonia. They chatted about the next game until the lights blinked out completely.

Antonia gasped and felt Skylar stand straight up. "NOT FUNNY, DEVILS," she said. The lights flicked back on, but no one was standing by the light switch.

Then a voice whispered, "Antoniaaaa." The hairs on the back of Antonia's neck stood up. Straight afterwards, she heard the same voice go, "Skylaaaar."

Skylar moved to the door and tried to open it – it was stuck. Antonia felt glued to her seat and couldn't move. After trying over and over again to open the door, Skylar came back to the bench and sat by Antonia, grabbing her arm. Antonia squeezed her back – it seemed to be the only movement her body would make.

The voice said, "You've been currrrssssssssed."

Antonia felt that cold feeling again, and she started shivering uncontrollably. "Who are you?" she asked, wildly.

Laughter travelled around them and now Antonia felt Skylar shiver.

"Not important," said the voice. "What's important is the curse."

Skylar swallowed and said, "What is the curse?"

The voice said, "Every one of your teammates will get hurt horribly, one by one, for the next seven days. They will never recover. Unlesssss. . ."

Skylar and Antonia looked at each other and gulped.

"Unless what?" Antonia finally said.

"Unless one of you hurts the other one in your next match," the voice said, then laughed so hard Antonia had to cover her ears.

Skylar stopped shivering. "Well, that's stupid," she said.

The voice was quiet.

"Antonia and I would never hurt each other. Ever. We're best friends."

Antonia felt herself nodding, though a tiny little something sprouted in her stomach. If it would stop the whole team from getting hurt, she wondered.

"Yeah," Antonia said, trying to make herself believe it.

The voice laughed. "You have the choice," it said. "Make it wisely."

The lights stopped flickering, and the coldness disappeared. Skylar and Antonia ran to the door and opened it, standing just outside and breathing in the air. Skylar turned to Antonia and looked at her fiercely. "I don't know what just happened, but I'm not going to hurt you, you understand? I think we should go and tell the coach."

Antonia nodded but didn't totally hear her. Instead, she was thinking about the next match and how she could protect her team. She swallowed and said, "You can trust me."

She heard a ghostly laugh behind her in the changing room, and the coldness spread all through her body.

OUIJA TERROR

BY BENJAMIN HARPER

Tisha had been looking forward to this weekend. She was spending the night over at her new best friend Sarah's house. Sarah had invited her other friends, Linda and Joy.

Tisha had just moved to this area at the beginning of the summer, and it had been hard for her to make friends at first. But then she'd met Sarah, and they'd hit it off straight away! Sarah had told her about Linda and Joy, and promised to introduce them. She said they would all be best friends.

Everyone had fun at the sleepover. Sarah's mum had made tacos for them. After dinner, they all watched videos and even sang some songs on Sarah's karaoke machine.

But then Sarah's mother told them it was time to go to bed. "You girls don't stay up too late," she warned. "But if you do, at least be quiet. I have to work tomorrow night."

Sarah's mother was a nurse at the local hospital, and had been working night shifts for the past few weeks. The girls promised they'd be quiet as they scrambled up the stairs to Sarah's room.

They spent the next hour or so texting friends and giggling. Tisha was having a great time, and she felt at home with Linda and Joy. Sarah had been right! She was really going to like living in this new area.

After texting got boring, Sarah tiptoed over

to her wardrobe. She got up on a chair and pulled an old box out from under a pile of jumpers.

"Do you want to have some fun?" she said, shuffling the box across the floor. She told them to come and sit around it in a circle.

"What is that thing?" Tisha asked, looking at the weird design on the front of the box. It looked kind of creepy!

"It's a Ouija board," Sarah said. "You can use it to talk to spirits. This was my sister's. My mum thinks we threw it away, but I sneaked it out of the rubbish. It's too cool not to keep!"

Sarah told the girls how to use it – two people sit on either side of the board with their fingers on a thing called a planchette. When a question is asked, the planchette moves across the board, either spelling out words using the alphabet, or pointing to "YES" or "NO".

She had used it lots of times, she said, and it was always fun.

Tisha was a little scared of it. She didn't like ghosts and didn't really want to talk to them! But after the other girls said they wanted to try it, she gave in.

To set the mood, Sarah lit a candle and turned off the lights. The girls all sat around the board, hoping someone would volunteer to go first.

"This is silly. I'll go!" Linda finally said, putting her fingers on the planchette. "Come on, Joy. We can do this." Joy shuffled closer and reached out towards the board.

"Hello, anyone there?" Linda called. "Come in! We wish to speak with you!" She giggled. She said she didn't believe in ghosts.

But then the planchette moved.

"Are you a good spirit or a bad spirit?" Linda

asked. Her fingers moved slowly in circles around the board. The other girls all watched in silence. Joy had been touching the planchette as well, but pulled her hands back when it started to move.

"That's creepy," she whispered. "It's moving on its own!"

The planchette moved over the board, slowly, slowly, aiming at letters.

"B," Linda said, reading the board. "A," she said, looking at the others. "D."

BAD.

At that moment, the lights flickered and the candle blew out.

Linda scooted away from the board, pushing it into the corner. "That's too scary," she cried. "I don't want to play any more!"

Nobody wanted to play any more, but the Ouija board hadn't finished yet. The board and planchette moved back into the middle of the girls' circle. They sat with their mouths open as it spelled word after word.

"You have awoken me from my slumber," the board spelled. "And now I will haunt you forever!"

The girls ran out of the room and down the stairs.

"What are we going to do?" Joy cried. "It's a real spirit!"

Tisha was shaking. She wished she hadn't come to this sleepover after all – now she was being hunted by a ghost!

A giant shadow formed on the wall behind them. What looked like fingers spread across the ceiling, reaching out towards the girls. Pictures fell off the wall, and what felt like a cold breeze blew through the room.

"We have to throw out the Ouija board," Sarah cried. "It's our only chance!"

They stumbled back up the stairs to her room. The board was there in the middle of the floor, the planchette spinning round and round.

"Grab it!" Sarah shouted. Tisha mustered up her courage and rushed into the room. She shoved the board and planchette back into the box. She ran back out, the box squirming in her arms like it was trying to escape.

The girls ran out to the rubbish bin and heaved a sigh of relief when Tisha flung the box inside, slamming the lid shut.

They went back in and collapsed in Sarah's room. "That was a close one," she said.

"I'll never say I don't believe in ghosts again," Linda added, "and I will never touch another Ouija board for as long as I live!"

They all fell asleep.

When they woke up the next morning, they were relieved they were all okay.

Sarah's mum had made them pancakes. They didn't laugh as much as they had before the Ouija board incident – they were all still pretty scared.

When Tisha left, Sarah said, "Everything is okay. The board is in the rubbish bin! The ghost can't get us as long as the board isn't here. I promise."

Tisha was relieved. As she walked home, she thought about her new friends. Even though they had been through that spooky experience, she was happy to make some new friends.

She decided not to tell her mum about what had happened. She would never be able to visit her new friends again! So she just said she'd had a fun time and went to dump her stuff in her room.

When she opened her door, she started screaming. There on her bed was…

The Ouija board.

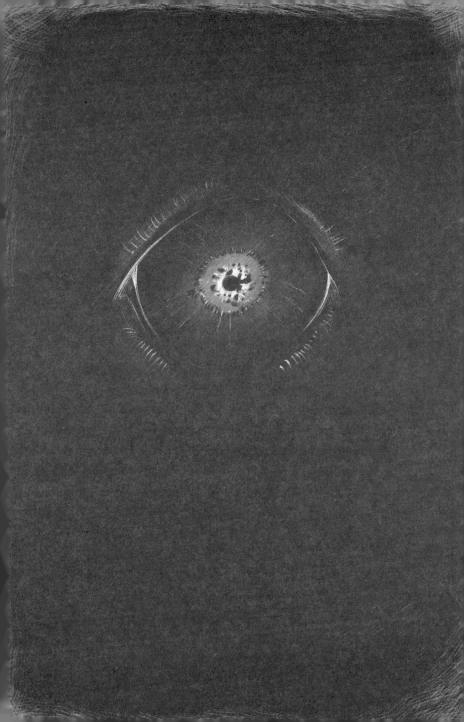

SECOND SIGHT

BY LAURIE S. SUTTON

Frank O'Neill knew it was bad news even before
the eye doctor said anything. He'd been having
trouble with his vision for a while now. And that was
in his one good eye.

"The old injury that blinded your left eye is
finally making you go blind in the right one," the
doctor said. "The damaged tissue is breaking down."

"Just great," Frank grumbled. "Now what am I
supposed to do?"

"You can have a cornea transplant," the doctor said. "It will replace the damaged cornea with a healthy one."

"Don't transplants come from dead people?" Frank shuddered.

"Don't worry," the doctor replied, laughing. "I've done hundreds of these surgeries, and none of the donors have come back to haunt me."

* * *

Frank was released from the hospital a day after the surgery and took the bus home. He looked over at the person sitting next to him. She held a scratch-card lottery ticket. He saw the numbers that had been revealed.

"Hey, you've won," Frank said.

"What?" the lady said, confused.

"You've won," Frank repeated.

He pointed at the card. Then he saw that it was unscratched.

The woman scratched the card with a coin, and Frank watched the winning numbers reveal themselves.

"Woo-hoo! I won a hundred pounds!" the woman shouted. "How did you know?"

Frank didn't answer. He didn't know. But somehow he'd seen it.

* * *

Frank immediately bought ten lottery scratch cards. He spread them out on the kitchen worktop at home. He could see all the numbers and symbols, even though he hadn't scratched off any of the boxes. He scratched the boxes with the highest winnings.

"Fifty pounds. Not much," Frank said. "I'll do better next time."

During the next week, Frank did do better.

He looked at each scratch card and only bought the ones he saw had the highest winnings. Frank soon raked in thousands of pounds.

The week after that, Frank decided to aim high. He wanted to win the One-Million-Pound game. Frank had to go into every shop all over the city to find a card that had that amount on it, but it was worth the effort. He pretended to be surprised when he scratched the card in the grocery shop.

Frank was on the local news that night. He got on the national news after he won three more big prizes. Frank soon moved into a luxury apartment. He stopped getting the bus. He had a private driver now.

One morning, a man came to Frank's door. He said his name was George and that he was the brother of the cornea donor. He had seen Frank on the news.

"I see you're using my sister's gift," George said.

"Yeah. I can see just fine now," Frank replied.

"I mean her gift of Second Sight," George corrected. "She was psychic and could see into the future. Her cornea transferred that gift to you, and you're using it to win the scratch-card lottery."

"Nah. I'm just lucky," Frank lied.

The brother stared Frank in the eye without speaking. It was intense, as if looking into Frank's soul.

"If you say so," George said. "Just don't get greedy."

As soon as the brother left Frank freaked out.

"He knows my secret!" Frank said. "If he tells anyone, they'll think I've cheated. I'll be banned from playing the lottery for life."

Frank couldn't take the chance that George wouldn't blab.

He had to make sure that he kept quiet. Permanently.

A few nights later, Frank secretly paid someone a large sum of money to kill George.

"Make it look like an accident," Frank said.

Two days later, Frank saw the news on TV about George having a terrible car accident. As Frank watched the news, there was a knock at his door. When Frank opened the door he saw George standing there. Frank thought he was seeing a ghost!

"I know what you did," George said. "My sister had Second Sight. But so do I. Your attempt to kill me failed because I literally saw it coming."

"What – what are you going to do?" Frank asked nervously.

"I'm not going to do anything," George replied. "But my sister is. Her spirit is very angry with you for trying to kill me."

Suddenly the vision in Frank's right eye clouded over. Then it went dark as the transplanted cornea failed completely.

"She is taking back the gift of sight from her cornea," George explained.

George left Frank to stumble around the fancy apartment. He was now blind in both eyes. Instead of having the gift of Second Sight, now he had no sight at all.

NIGHT VISITORS

BY MICHAEL DAHL

Two beams of light streamed through the forest. Jack and Arlo were shining their torches through the dark bushes and trees.

"Ugh! Aim your torch down on the ground," said Arlo. "I just tripped over a root or something."

"Quiet!" said Jack. In his creepiest voice, he added, "We don't want the ghosts to hear us. Mwah ha ha!"

"Can we please not talk about that kind of stuff," muttered Arlo. "We're only doing this because –" He froze. One of their torches had picked out something odd among the shadowy, crowded trees. Something grey and flat and worn.

"That's it," whispered Jack.

A small house, more like a cabin, sat quietly in the dark. Its walls were grey with age and covered with moss. The warped and bumpy tiles on its roof reminded Arlo of blistered skin. In fact, the entire house, its black silhouette beneath the trees, made Arlo think of a giant, squatting toad.

"Go on," said Jack, more loudly this time.

"You go on," said Arlo.

Neither boy moved. "If we don't go inside, the guys will know we've chickened out," said Jack. "There's supposed to be a piece of paper pinned to one of the walls in there. We have to bring it back."

"Yeah! Well, Darwin won't be bringing it back," Arlo pointed out.

Darwin was the third member of their team. He had stayed back at the campsite. Jack and Arlo told him the other guys would kick him off the football team if he refused to complete the stupid dare. "I don't care," Darwin had said. "There's something wrong about this place. I'll tell the guys tomorrow that I didn't go with you. I don't care."

"We'll say you came with us," offered Jack.

"No, that would be lying," said Darwin. Arlo totally agreed. If you don't do the dare, you're done. You're out. So sad, but that's the way life worked.

Gripping their torches tightly, the two boys crept forwards. A wall of human-sized bushes surrounded the house, their sharp branches reaching out. The boys moved slowly but were soon within a few metres of the front door. It sagged off its hinges and swung gently in a sudden breeze.

"What's that?" asked Arlo.

A snapping sound had broken the silence.

The sound came from behind the swinging door.

"Maybe it's the little old man and lady who used to live here," said Jack. That was the local story anyway.

"No more of the ghost stuff," said Arlo. "I'm creeped out enough, okay?"

Squeeeeeeak.

The door was swinging faster. There must have been a breeze blowing inside the house through the broken windows. With another loud snap, the door fell off its hinges. The boys cried out. "Arlo," said Jack. His voice was quivering. "Do you see —? G-g-ghosts!"

Arlo trained his beam upwards from the ground till it shone on the door. Or, rather, on the black hole left behind by the fallen door. The darkness seemed to be moving. Two greyish blobs floated above the floor, hovering inside the dark house.

"Maybe that's from the Moon," said Jack.

"There ain't no Moon," said Arlo, between gritted teeth.

The grey blobs grew slightly larger. They seemed to be moving closer to the doorframe. The boys felt ice cubes sliding down their spines. Hair stood up on their arms. Their feet froze to the ground. The grey blobs came out of the doorway. The boys could see two grey round heads. Two old people, a man and woman, stepped forwards, arm in arm. Their faces were creased and wrinkled like the bark on the nearby trees. Their black eyes glittered in the torches. Black as crows' eyes.

Then, the old man and woman each lifted an arm. They smiled and waved at the boys. Their mouths stretched wide like toads.

"Run!" screamed Arlo.

They turned and scrambled past the thick bushes. The sharp branches scraped at their arms and bare legs, drawing blood. The beams from the twin torches bobbed up and down as they raced between the trees.

"Darwin! Darwin!" they yelled. Behind the running boys, in the dark forest, there was only silence.

In a few minutes, they reached the campsite. Arlo and Jack bent over, hands on their knees, catching their breath. "Who were those creepy people?" gasped Arlo.

"I don't care," said Jack. "We're getting out of here."

Jack stood up. "Darwin," he called again. "C'mon. We're leaving."

Darwin didn't respond. The boys decided he must be asleep, but then they heard the zipper on the front flap of the tent. It unzipped all the way round to widen the doorway.

"Darwin?" asked Arlo.

It wasn't Darwin. The old man and woman pushed aside the tent flaps and stood there. They waved again. And smiled. This time the boys noticed their tiny, jagged teeth. Their long, sharp fingernails. Behind the old, toad-like couple, the two boys saw Darwin's socks and shoes lying on the floor, next to the T-shirt he always wore to bed.

IT'S A TRAP

BY MEGAN ATWOOD

Revenge. It was the only thing Malik could think about.

He walked home from school steaming from the practical joke his new friends had played on him. During PE, they'd taken out his white uniform shirt and stained it with ketchup. Only, they made the stains read, "I eat poo". He got into trouble with his teacher and the headteacher for that one. He didn't grass on his friends, though, so they all gathered around him and clapped him on the back afterwards. He knew as the new kid at the school he might get some teasing. He just didn't think it would be from his new friends.

But his new town was just different.

And so was his home. He walked up the front steps of his huge Victorian house. He had loved it when they first moved in. But now a few weeks later, things had been weird. . . He took a deep breath and opened the door. He stepped into the hall and threw his backpack down, sprinting up the stairs to change his shirt before one of his dads saw him in it.

Somehow it was always cold in the house. He changed out of his school uniform and came back down the stairs, joining one of his dads in the kitchen for a snack.

"Hey, Malik, how was school?" his dad asked, chewing on a biscuit he'd clearly just made.

Malik shrugged and grabbed a biscuit. He wasn't about to tell his dad the truth about the day.

"Did you happen to move the table downstairs from the dining room to the living room?" his dad asked.

Malik stopped chewing. "No," he said.

His dad shook his head. "So weird. For a week or so, things around the house have been moved to different places. Are you SURE it's not you?" He fixed Malik with a hard stare.

"It's not me!" Malik said. But then his heart sank. Was it possible his new "friends" had started playing pranks on him in his own home? He cleared his throat. "When did you first start noticing that things were getting moved?"

His dad said, "Probably two weeks ago." His dad shrugged and laughed a little. "Maybe this place is haunted."

Malik swallowed. Right when he'd started to be friends with all of them. "That's weird," he said, and went back upstairs, wondering what he could do.

The next morning, Malik woke up to a yell from one of his dads. He sprinted downstairs and stared in disbelief. Their living room was a mess — there were papers everywhere, paintings were squint and there were weird liquid stains on the sofas. But worse, on one of the walls, "GET OUT" was written in what looked like blood.

Malik fumed. He knew it had to be his friends. The thought of revenge popped into his mind again. He had to think of a way to get back at them.

At school, he didn't say anything to them and just watched as they jostled each other and said rude things. His friend Daniel said, "That was fun last night, guys."

Malik stopped in his tracks. "What did you do last night?" he asked, hoping to sound casual.

They just laughed and Rick said, "Maybe soon you can join us. But now you don't need to know." Malik had an idea of what they'd done.

When he got home that day, he'd worked out his plan. He wouldn't grass on them, but he could trap them so that his dads could see who was behind everything. He knew just how to do it too.

Down in the basement of the house, there was a door that led to what used to be a coal room. The place was dank and dark, and Malik had only been in there once – and once was enough. If he could lure them through that door, he could trap them there and make them pay.

He would simply stay up and wait for them to come into his house, then tell them he had a great idea to continue the prank. In the basement. In the coal room. And then he'd shut them in there and lock the door.

When his dads went to bed, Malik sneaked down into the living room to wait for his friends. He tried to stay awake but soon he dozed off, listening to the ticking of the clock.

Something jarred Malik awake, and when he looked at the clock it was midnight.

The living room windows shone with moonlight and Malik listened carefully. He heard a thump in the kitchen and he sat straight up. Something moved across the floor, like someone was moving furniture. His friends were here.

He tiptoed to the kitchen but when he got there, no one was there. The stove had been moved out, but that was it. Then he saw it – a glowing light coming from behind the cracked basement door.

They must have gone down to the basement. The light disappeared and Malik scurried to the door. The light glowed at the bottom of the steps and kept moving. Malik quietly walked down the stairs, following. He couldn't believe how quiet they were being. The light hovered around the old coal room and Malik almost gasped.

They had found it somehow. The light disappeared into the room and Malik followed.

The room dripped with something, but the light hovered there. Malik took a deep breath to tell his friends off, but then he realized that no one was in there with him. The room was empty. Sweat trickled down his temples and his knees started shaking.

"Who . . . who are you?" he whispered to the light.

The light blinked out. And at that very moment the door to the coal room slammed with a bang. Malik heard the key in the lock and knew he was stuck there with whatever else had found the room.

GLOSSARY

CORNEA coating of the eyeball that covers the iris and pupil and lets light through

HIDEOUS horribly ugly or disgusting

MUSTER stir up or bring to action

PLANCHETTE small, triangular or heart-shaped board supported on casters at two points and a vertical pencil at a third, believed to produce automatic writing when lightly touched by the fingers

PRESENCE something felt or believed to be present, like a spirit

REVENGE punishing or hurting someone who has done you wrong

SILHOUETTE outline of a dark shape seen against a pale background

TRANSPLANT transfer an organ or tissue from one person to another person

VICTORIAN typical of literature, art and tastes of the the time during the reign of Queen Victoria

VOW promise to do something

DISCUSSION QUESTIONS

1. What is your favourite story in this book?
   Discuss why you liked that particular story so
   much.
2. What makes a scary story so creepy? Talk about
   two or three things (blood, monsters, ghosts or
   other) that scare your socks off!
3. Discuss some of the different ways in which
   monsters were portrayed in these stories. How
   were they different? How were they similar?
   Use examples from the book.

WRITING PROMPTS

1. Write another ghost story. How will you make
   your story different from the ones included in
   this book?
2. Write a second part, or sequel, to one of the
   stories in this book. What happens next?
   You decide!
3. Create a list of your biggest fears, such as
   ghosts, monsters or the dark. Then write down
   how you might be able to overcome these fears.

ABOUT THE AUTHORS

BENJAMIN HARPER

Benjamin Harper lives in Los Angeles, USA, where he edits superhero books for a living. When he's not at work, he writes, watches horror films and hangs out with his cats Marjorie and Jerry, a betta fish called Toby and a tank full of four rough-skinned newts. He tends a bog garden full of carnivorous plants and also grows milkweed to help save Monarch butterflies. His other books include the Bug Girl series, *Obsessed With Star Wars*, *Star Wars: Rolling with BB-8!*, *Hansel & Gretel & Zombies* and many more.

LAURIE S. SUTTON

Laurie Sutton is a comic book writer and editor. She is also the author of *The Mystery of the Aztec Tomb* and *The Secret of the Sea Creature* from the You Choose Stories: Scooby-Doo! series. She currently lives in Florida, USA.

MICHAEL DAHL

Michael Dahl is the prolific author of more than 200 books for children and young adults. He has won the AEP Distinguished Achievement Award three times for his non-fiction, a Teacher's Choice award from *Learning* magazine and a Seal of Excellence from the Creative Child Awards. Dahl currently lives in Minneapolis, Minnesota, USA.

MEGAN ATWOOD

Megan Atwood is a writer and professor with over 45 books published. She lives in New Jersey, USA, where she wrangles cats, dreams up ridiculous stories and thinks of ways to make children laugh all day.

READ ALL FOUR

GHOST STORIES
TO SCARE YOUR SOCKS OFF!
— ATWOOD · DAHL · HARPER · SUTTON —

MONSTER STORIES
TO SCARE YOUR SOCKS OFF!
— ATWOOD · DAHL · HARPER · SUTTON —

SORCERY STORIES
TO SCARE YOUR SOCKS OFF!
— ATWOOD · DAHL · HARPER · SUTTON —

ZOMBIE STORIES
TO SCARE YOUR SOCKS OFF!
— ATWOOD · DAHL · HARPER · SUTTON —